The Feelings Book

 TODD PARR

L B

LITTLE, BROWN AND COMPANY
New York Boston

ABDO
Spotlight

ABDOBOOKS.COM

Reinforced library bound edition published in 2020 by Spotlight, a division of ABDO, PO Box 398166, Minneapolis, Minnesota 55439. Spotlight produces high-quality reinforced library bound editions for schools and libraries. Published by agreement with Little, Brown and Company.

Printed in the United States of America, North Mankato, Minnesota.
042019
092019

THIS BOOK CONTAINS
RECYCLED MATERIALS

L B LITTLE, BROWN

Hachette Book Group
237 Park Avenue, New York, NY 10017

Little, Brown and Company is a division of Hachette Book Group, Inc.
The Little, Brown name and logo are trademarks of Hachette Book Group, Inc.

First Paperback Edition: April 2009
Originally published in hardcover in September 2000 by Little, Brown and Company.

Library of Congress Control Number: 2019930052

Publisher's Cataloging-in-Publication Data

Names: Parr, Todd, author. | Parr, Todd, illustrator.
Title: The feelings book / by Todd Parr; illustrated by Todd Parr.
Description: Minneapolis, Minnesota : Spotlight, 2020. | Series: Todd Parr picture books
Summary: This title features a wide range of emotions we all experience and how to discuss them.
Identifiers: ISBN 9781532143717 (lib. bdg.)
Subjects: LCSH: Feelings--Juvenile fiction. | Emotions--Juvenile fiction. | Mood (Psychology)--Juvenile fiction. | Happiness--Juvenile fiction. | Anger--Juvenile fiction. | Sadness--Juvenile fiction.
Classification: DDC [E]--dc23

Spotlight

A Division of ABDO
abdobooks.com

This book is dedicated to
Dad, Tammy, Sandy, Sara, Dawn, Bryan, Bill,
Candy, Jerry, Liz and Gerry, John and Linda
Alioto, Maggie W., Jeff and Steve, Jim and
Jean, Bully, Mow, Isabel and Benny, Michael,
Artt, Megan, Cindy Sue, Kerri, Stacey, Linda,
and everyone at Little, Brown.

Love,
Todd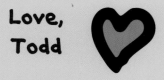

Sometimes I feel silly

Sometimes I feel cranky

Sometimes I feel scared

Sometimes I feel like standing on my head

Sometimes I feel like reading a book under the covers

Sometimes I feel like celebrating my birthday

even though
it's not today

Sometimes I feel brave

Sometimes I feel like looking out the window all day

Sometimes I feel

Sometimes I feel like making mudpies

Sometimes I feel like
I have a tummy ache

Sometimes I feel like holding hands with a friend

Sometimes I feel lonely

Sometimes I feel like staying in the bathtub all day

Sometimes I feel like trying something new

Sometimes I feel like dressing up

Sometimes I feel

like doing nothing

Sometimes I feel like camping with my dog

Sometimes I feel like crying

Sometimes I feel like eating pizza for breakfast

Sometimes I feel like kissing a sea lion

Sometimes I feel
like a king

No matter how
you feel, don't
keep your feelings
to yourself.
Share them with
Someone you love.

Love,
Todd